HILLTOP ELEMENTARY SCHOOL

W9-BKY-226

HILLTOP ELEMENTARY SCHOOL

James AND THE Rain

BY Karla Kuskin

ILLUSTRATED BY

Reg Cartwright

SIMON & SCHUSTER BOOKS FOR YOUNG READERS

SIMON & SCHUSTER BOOKS FOR YOUNG READERS
An imprint of Simon & Schuster Children's Publishing Division
1230 Avenue of the Americas, New York, New York 10020
Text copyright © 1957, 1995 by Karla Kuskin
Illustrations copyright © 1995 by Reg Cartwright
All rights reserved including the right of reproduction
in whole or in part in any form.
Originally published in 1957 by Harper and Brothers Publishers
with illustrations by Karla Kuskin.
SIMON & SCHUSTER BOOKS FOR YOUNG READERS
is a trademark of Simon & Schuster.
Book design by Paul Zakris.
The text for this book is set in 14-point Korinna.
The illustrations were done in oil paint.
Manufactured in the United States of America.
10 9 8 7 6 5 4 3 2 1

Library of Congress Cataloging-in-Publication Data
Kuskin, Karla.
James and the rain / by Karla Kuskin ;
illustrated by Reg Cartwright. p. cm.
Summary: James puts on his yellow slicker and goes out
into the rain to play rainy day games with an ever-
increasing number of different animals.
1. Animals—Fiction. [1. Rain and rainfall—Fiction. 2. Counting—
Fiction. 3. Stories in rhyme.] I. Cartwright, Reg, ill. II. Title.
PZ8.3.K96Jam   1995   [E]—dc20   93-49345 CIP AC
ISBN: 0-671-88808-0

For Caroline, Madeleine, and Jake in the rain
—K. K.

For my mother, 1910-1994
—R. C.

James pressed his nose against the pane

and saw a million drops of rain.

The earth was wet,

the sky was gray,

it looked like it would rain all day.

James had a very yellow coat

that buttoned to his chin,

he had a pair of rubber boots

to tuck his trousers in.

He took a big umbrella

from the big umbrella stand,

he buttoned up his yellow coat

and looked extremely grand.

He opened his umbrella
with the handle made of cane,
he pulled his yellow hat down tight
and stepped into the rain.
James ambled through the wet green grass
under the wet gray sky,
the rain rained everywhere he went
but James stayed warm and dry.

Out in a meadow of clover and grain

a cow munched her lunch

and gazed at the rain.

"What do you do in the rain?" said James.

"Do you have any excellent rainy day games?"

"I do," said the cow,

"for I love the rain

and the sound it makes on the leaves and grain.

I always stand under a very large tree

and let the rain fall on the leaves and me."

Then James and the cow stood side by side

and the rain came down

on the cow's brown hide.

"Cow," said James,

"if I'm not wrong,

it might be nice if we strolled along."

So they strolled along till they met two ducks . . .

"What do you do in the rain?" said James.

"Do you have any excellent rainy day games?"

"We do," snapped the ducks

in small short quacks,

"we love the rain as it falls on our backs.

We flap our feathers

and flitter around

making a rackety quackety sound."

Then all of them flittered

and gave loud quacks

and the rain rained down on all of their backs.

"Ducks," mooed the cow,

"if I'm not wrong,

it might be nice if we strolled along."

So they strolled along till they met three toads . . .

"What do you do in the rain?" said James.

"Do you have any excellent rainy day games?"

"We love the rain," croaked the three fat toads,

"and the puddles of mud that it makes in the roads.

From puddle to puddle we scuddle and jump,

we land in the mud with a thud and a thump.

Come jump with us all."

So they all of them jumped,

they all of them scuddled,

and all of them thumped.

(A scuddle is the short, sticky run from one

mud puddle to the next.)

"Toads," quacked the ducks,

"if we're not wrong,

it might be nice if we strolled along."

So they strolled along till they met four birds . . .

"What do you do in the rain?" said James.

"Do you have any excellent rainy day games?"

"Well," said the birds,

"when it rains we soar

up to the clouds and a little bit more.

We seek and we search

soaking our skins

to try to find out where the rain begins."

So all of them tried to soar to the sky

but only the birds got a little bit high.

"Birds," croaked the toads,

"if we're not wrong,

it might be nice if we strolled along."

So they strolled along till they met five dogs . . .

"What do you do in the rain?" said James.

"Do you have any excellent rainy day games?"

"Rowf," said the dogs and began to bark,

"we love the rain

it's a marvelous lark.

We crash and we splash and we slip on stones,

we scurry and hurry to bury our bones.

We stick out our tongues as we scamper around,

and drink down the rain with a glunking sound."

(Glunk is the sound everybody makes

when they drink in a hurry. You glunk.)

So all of them stuck their tongues way out

and the rain was so cold that they had to shout.

"Dogs," chirped the birds,

"if we're not wrong,

it might be nice if we strolled along."

So they strolled along till they met six rabbits . . .

"What do you do in the rain?" said James.

"Do you have any excellent rainy day games?"

"Oh," said the rabbits and nibbled their lettuce,

"we like the rain if it doesn't wet us.

We race in the rain right out of our hutches,

we run so fast that the rain can't touch us."

So everyone raced with their might and main,

trying to dodge the drops of rain

(but nobody did).

Then the dogs barked,

"Rabbits, if we're not wrong,

it might be nice if we strolled along."

So they strolled along till they met seven mice . . .

"What do you do in the rain?" said James.

"Do you have any excellent rainy day games?"

"Oh," squeaked the mice

who were terribly shy,

"we like the rain

if our ears stay dry.

We pick red flowers

out of their beds

and wear them as hats

to cover our heads."

Then they all picked flowers just like the mice

and wore them as hats and looked very nice.

Then the rabbits peeped,

"Mice, if we're not wrong,

it might be nice if we strolled along."

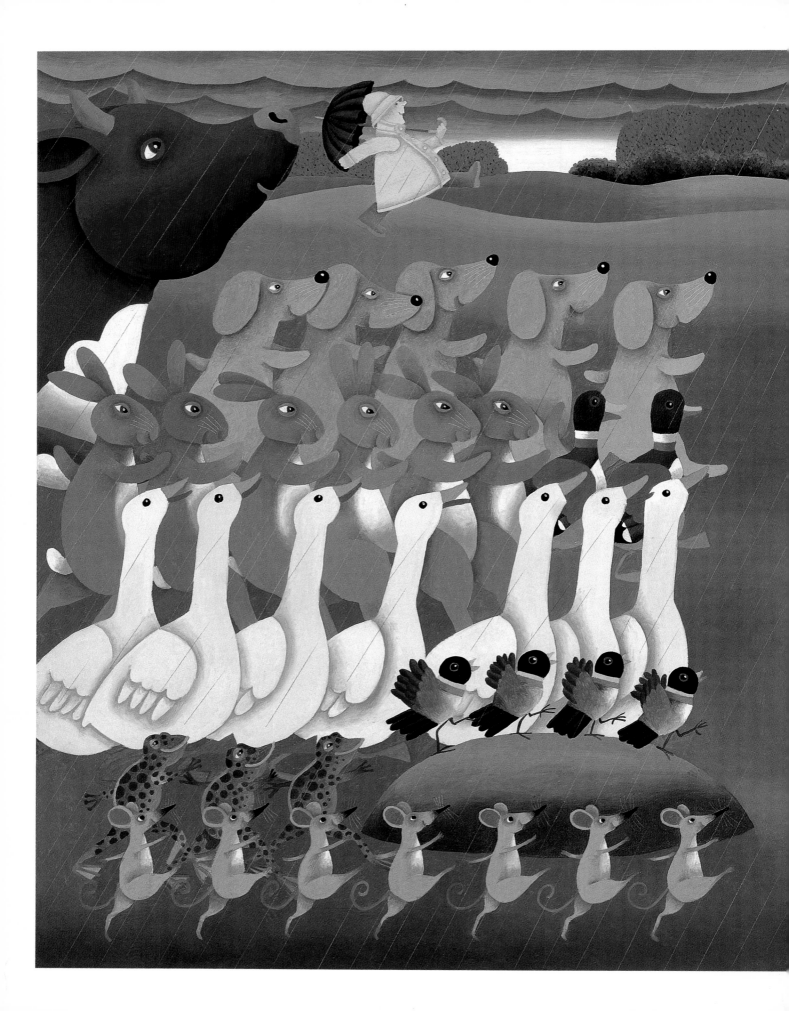

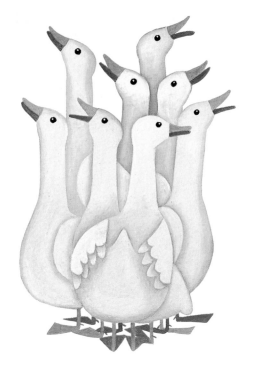

So they strolled along till they met eight geese . . .

"What do you do in the rain?" said James.

"Do you have any excellent rainy day games?"

"Honk," honked the geese

with a high goose cry,

"we march through the drops

but we stay quite dry.

With our wonderful down

and oil in our feathers,

we're warmer than toast

in the wildest of weathers."

So everyone marched

from pillar to post

but only the geese

stayed warmer than toast.

Then the mice squeaked,

"Geese, if we're not wrong,

it might be nice if we strolled along."

So they strolled along till they met nine pigs . . .

"What do you do in the rain?" said James.

"Do you have any excellent rainy day games?"

"Oink," oinked the pigs,

"yes indeed we do.

We play rain games

till the rain is through.

We kerplunk in the mud

and then we kerplosh,

we get so muddy

we have to wash.

So they rolled in the mud

and ran mud races

and when they had finished

they washed their faces.

Then the geese honked,

"Pigs, if we're not wrong,

it might be nice if we strolled along."

So they strolled along till they met ten cats . . .

"What do you do in the rain?" said James.

"Do you have any excellent rainy day games?"

"Meow," mewed the cats,

"we like the rain

and the sound that it makes

on the windowpane.

But best of all

as the wind howls higher,

we like to sit by a roaring fire."

So they went inside and sat by the fire.
The rain came down
and the wind howled higher.
And that is the end.
It rained and it poured,
they all fell asleep
and all of them snored.